Winter Bible School

"Have a nice nap?" inquired Jerry, with a broad grin. FRONTISPIECE. *See page 3.*

The Adventures of Grandfather Frog

THORNTON W. BURGESS

Original Illustrations by Harrison Cady
Adapted by Thea Kliros

PUBLISHED IN ASSOCIATION WITH THE
THORNTON W. BURGESS MUSEUM AND THE
GREEN BRIAR NATURE CENTER, SANDWICH, MASSACHUSETTS,
BY
DOVER PUBLICATIONS, INC., NEW YORK

DOVER CHILDREN'S THRIFT CLASSICS
EDITOR: PHILIP SMITH

Copyright © 1992 by Dover Publications, Inc.
All rights reserved.

This Dover edition, first published in 1992 in association with the Thornton W. Burgess Museum and the Green Briar Nature Center, Sandwich, Massachusetts, who have provided a new introduction, is an unabridged republication of the edition published by Little, Brown, and Company, Boston, in 1915. The original Harrison Cady illustrations have been adapted for this new edition by Thea Kliros.

Library of Congress Cataloging-in-Publication Data

Burgess, Thornton W. (Thornton Waldo), 1874–1965.
    The adventures of Grandfather Frog / Thornton W. Burgess ; original illustrations by Harrison Cady, adapted by Thea Kliros.
        p.   cm. — (Dover children's thrift classics)
    "Published in association with the Thornton W. Burgess Museum and the Green Briar Nature Center, Sandwich, Massachusetts."
    Summary: Chronicles the adventures of Grandfather Frog and his animal friends.
    ISBN-13: 978-0-486-27400-3 (pbk.)
    ISBN-10: 0-486-27400-4 (pbk.)
    [1. Frogs—Fiction. 2. Animals—Fiction.] I. Cady, Harrison, 1877– ill. II. Kliros, Thea, ill. III. Title. IV. Series.
PZ7.B917Abm 1992
[Fic]—dc20   92–13146
                                                                    CIP
                                                                    AC

Manufactured in the United States by Courier Corporation
27400414
www.doverpublications.com

Introduction to the Dover Edition

THORNTON W. BURGESS was born January 14, 1874, in Sandwich, Massachusetts, a Cape Cod town known for glass manufacture. As a young boy, Thornton found adventure and solace in nature and all it offered. He passed on his own love of the outdoors to his son through the magic tales that he created. He was encouraged by Little, Brown, and Company to publish these stories. *Old Mother West Wind*, his first children's book, was introduced in 1910. Mr. Burgess interested both children and adults in nature by bringing animal characters to life and putting them into exciting situations. Peter Rabbit was Burgess' most famous character.

Today, the Thornton W. Burgess Society continues to carry out the philosophies of Thornton W. Burgess' stories. The Society operates the Green Briar Nature Center and the Thornton W. Burgess Museum in Sandwich, Massachusetts, and publishes periodic newsletters and bulletins to inspire reverence for wildlife and concern for the natural environment. The Society is a leading force in environmental education on Cape Cod.

Grandfather Frog has a very big mouth! He does not mind being teased about it since a big mouth comes in very handy for catching tasty green flies. In this collection of stories, however, Grandfather Frog's big mouth gets him into a lot of trouble. Learn more about his adventures and meet some of his friends that live around the Smiling Pool. When you visit a "smiling pool" where you live, listen carefully for Grandfather Frog. His "chug-arum" is unmistakable! *The Adventures of Grandfather Frog* was first published in 1915. The stories in this book have timeless appeal for children of all ages.

Contents

Contents

List of Illustrations

viii

I
Billy Mink Finds
Little Joe Otter

BILLY MINK ran around the edge of the Smiling Pool and turned down by the Laughing Brook. His eyes twinkled with mischief, and he hurried as only Billy can. As he passed Jerry Muskrat's house, Jerry saw him.

"Hi, Billy Mink! Where are you going in such a hurry this fine morning?" he called.

"To find Little Joe Otter. Have you seen anything of him?" replied Billy.

"No," said Jerry. "He's probably down to the Big River fishing. I heard him say last night that he was going."

"Thanks," said Billy Mink, and without waiting to say more he was off like a little brown flash.

Jerry watched him out of sight. "Hump!" exclaimed Jerry. "Billy Mink is in a terrible hurry this morning. Now I wonder what he is so anxious to find Little Joe Otter for. When

1

they get their heads together, it is usually for some mischief."

Jerry climbed to the top of his house and looked over the Smiling Pool in the direction from which Billy Mink had just come. Almost at once he saw Grandfather Frog fast asleep on his big green lily-pad. The legs of a foolish green fly were sticking out of one corner of his big mouth. Jerry couldn't help laughing, for Grandfather Frog certainly did look funny.

"He's had a good breakfast this morning, and his full stomach has made him sleepy," thought Jerry. "But he's getting careless in his old age. He certainly is getting careless. The idea of going to sleep right out in plain sight like that!"

Suddenly a new thought popped into his head. "Billy Mink saw him, and that is why he is so anxious to find Little Joe Otter. He is planning to play some trick on Grandfather Frog as sure as pollywogs have tails!" exclaimed Jerry. Then his eyes began to twinkle as he added: "I think I'll have some fun myself."

Without another word Jerry slipped down into the water and swam over to the big green lily-pad of Grandfather Frog. Then he hit the water a smart blow with his tail. Grandfather Frog's big goggly eyes flew open, and he was just about to make a frightened plunge into the Smiling Pool when he saw Jerry.

"Have a nice nap?" inquired Jerry, with a broad grin.

"I wasn't asleep!" protested Grandfather Frog indignantly. "I was just thinking."

"Don't you think it a rather dangerous plan to think so long with your eyes closed?" asked Jerry.

"Well, maybe I did just doze off," admitted Grandfather Frog sheepishly.

"Maybe you did," replied Jerry. "Now listen." Then Jerry whispered in Grandfather Frog's ear, and both chuckled as if they were enjoying some joke, for they are great friends, you know. Afterward Jerry swam back to his house, and Grandfather Frog closed his eyes so as to look just as he did when he was asleep.

Meanwhile Billy Mink had hurried down the Laughing Brook. Half-way to the Big River he met Little Joe Otter bringing home a big fish, for you know Little Joe is a great fisherman. Billy Mink hastened to tell him how Grandfather Frog had fallen fast asleep on his big green lily-pad.

"It's a splendid chance to have some fun with Grandfather Frog and give him a great scare," concluded Billy.

Little Joe Otter put his fish down and grinned. He likes to play pranks almost as well as he likes to go fishing.

"What can we do?" said he.

"I've thought of a plan," replied Billy. "Do you happen to know where we can find Longlegs the Blue Heron?"

"Yes," said Little Joe. "I saw him fishing not five minutes ago."

Then Billy told Little Joe his plan, and laughing and giggling, the two little scamps hurried off to find Longlegs the Blue Heron.

II

Longlegs the Blue Heron
Receives Callers

LONGLEGS THE BLUE HERON felt decidedly out of sorts. It was a beautiful morning, too beautiful for any one to be feeling that way. Indeed, it was the same beautiful morning in which Grandfather Frog had caught so many foolish green flies.

Jolly, round, bright Mr. Sun was smiling his broadest. The Merry Little Breezes of Old

Mother West Wind were dancing happily here and there over the Green Meadows, looking for some good turn to do for others. The little feathered people to whom Old Mother Nature has given the great blessing of music in their throats were pouring out their sweetest songs. So it seemed as if there was no good reason why Longlegs should feel out of sorts. The fact is the trouble with Longlegs was an empty stomach. Yes, Sir, that is what ailed Longlegs the Blue Heron that sunshiny morning. You know it is hard work to be hungry and happy at the same time.

So Longlegs stood on the edge of a shallow little pool in the Laughing Brook, grumbling to himself. Just a little while before, he had seen Little Joe Otter carrying home a big fish, and this had made him hungrier and more out of sorts than ever. In the first place it made him envious, and envy, you know, always stirs up bad feelings. He knew perfectly well that Little Joe had got that fish by boldly chasing it until he caught it, for Little Joe can swim even faster than a fish. But Longlegs chose to try to make himself think that it was all luck. Moreover, he wanted to blame some one for his own lack of success, as most people who fail do. So when Little Joe had called out: "Hi, Longlegs, what luck this fine morning?" Longlegs just pretended not to hear. But when Little Joe was out of sight and hearing, he began to grumble to himself.

"No wonder I have no luck with that fellow racing up and down the Laughing Brook," said he. "He isn't content to catch what he wants himself, but frightens the rest of the fish so that an honest fisherman like me has no chance at all. I don't see what Old Mother Nature was thinking of when she gave him a liking for fish. He and Billy Mink are just two worthless little scamps, born to make trouble for other people."

He was still grumbling when these two same little scamps poked their heads out of the grass on the other side of the little pool. "You look happy, Longlegs. Must be that you have had a good breakfast," said Little Joe, nudging Billy Mink.

Longlegs snapped his great bill angrily. "What are you doing here, spoiling my fishing?" he demanded. "Haven't you got the Big River and all the rest of the Laughing Brook to fool around in? This is my pool, and I'll thank you to keep away!"

Billy Mink chuckled so that Longlegs heard him, and that didn't improve his temper a bit. But before he could say anything more, Little Joe Otter spoke.

"Thank you," said Longlegs. "I believe I have an errand up that way." *Page 8.*

"Oh," said he, "we beg your pardon. We just happen to know that Grandfather Frog is sound asleep, and we thought that if you hadn't had good luck this morning, you might like to know about it. As long as you think so ill of us, we'll just run over and tell Blackcap the Night Heron."

Little Joe turned as if to start off in search of Blackcap at once. "Hold on a minute!" called Longlegs, and tried to make his voice sound pleasant, a difficult thing to do, because, you know, his voice is very harsh and disagreeable. "The truth is, I haven't had a mouthful of breakfast and to be hungry is apt to make me cross. Where did you say Grandfather Frog is?"

"I didn't say," replied Little Joe, "but if you really want to know, he is sitting on his big green lily-pad in the Smiling Pool fast asleep right in plain sight."

"Thank you," said Longlegs. "I believe I have an errand up that way, now I think of it. I believe I'll just go over and have a look at him. I have never seen him asleep."

III
Longlegs Visits the Smiling Pool

LONGLEGS THE BLUE HERON watched
Billy Mink and Little Joe Otter disappear
down the Laughing Brook. As long as they
were in sight, he sat without moving, his head
drawn down between his shoulders just as if
he had nothing more important to think about
than a morning nap. But if you had been near
enough to have seen his keen eyes, you would
never have suspected him of even thinking of
a nap. Just as soon as he felt sure that the two
little brown-coated scamps were out of sight,
he stretched his long neck up until he was
almost twice as tall as he had been a minute
before. He looked this way and that way to
make sure that no danger was near, spread his
great wings, flapped heavily up into the air,
and then, with his head once more tucked
back between his shoulders and his long legs
straight out behind him, he flew out over the
Green Meadows, and making a big circle,
headed straight for the Smiling Pool.

All this time Billy Mink and Little Joe Otter
had not been so far away as Longlegs sup-

posed. They had been hiding where they could watch him, and the instant he spread his wings, they started back up the Laughing Brook towards the Smiling Pool to see what would happen there. You see they knew perfectly well that Longlegs was flying up to the Smiling Pool in the hope that he could catch Grandfather Frog for his breakfast. They didn't really mean that any harm should come to Grandfather Frog, but they meant that he should have a great fright. You see, they were like a great many other people, so heedless and thoughtless that they thought it fun to frighten others.

"Of course we'll waken Grandfather Frog in time for him to get away with nothing more than a great scare," said Little Joe Otter, as they hurried along. "It will be such fun to see his big goggly eyes pop out when he opens them and sees Longlegs just ready to gobble him up! And won't Longlegs be hopping mad when we cheat him out of the breakfast he is so sure he is going to have!"

They reached the Smiling Pool before Longlegs, who had taken a roundabout way, and they hid among the bulrushes where they could see and not be seen.

"There's the old fellow just as I left him, fast asleep," whispered Billy Mink.

Sure enough, there on his big green lily-pad sat Grandfather Frog with his eyes shut. At least, they seemed to be shut. And over on top of his big house sat Jerry Muskrat. Jerry seemed to be too busy opening a fresh-water clam to notice anything else; but the truth is he was watching all that was going on. You see, he had suspected that Billy Mink was going to play some trick on Grandfather Frog, so he had warned him. When he had seen Longlegs coming towards the Smiling Pool, he had given Grandfather Frog another warning, and he knew that now he was only pretending to be asleep.

Straight up to the Smiling Pool came Longlegs the Blue Heron, and on the very edge of it, among the bulrushes, he dropped his long legs and stood with his toes in the water, his long neck stretched up so that he could look all over the Smiling Pool. There, just as Little Joe Otter had said, sat Grandfather Frog on his big green lily-pad, fast asleep. At least, he seemed to be fast asleep. The eyes of Longlegs sparkled with hunger and the thought of what a splendid breakfast Grandfather Frog would make. Very slowly, putting each foot down as carefully as he knew how, Longlegs began to walk along the shore so as to get opposite the big green lily-pad where Grand-

father Frog was sitting. And over in the bulrushes on the other side, Little Joe Otter and
Billy Mink nudged each other and clapped
their hands over their mouths to keep from
laughing aloud.

IV

The Patience of
Longlegs the Blue Heron

Patience often wins the day
When over-haste has lost the way.

IF THERE IS one virtue which Longlegs the
Heron possesses above another it is
patience. Yes, Sir, Longlegs certainly has got
patience. He believes that if a thing is worth
having, it is worth waiting for, and that if he
waits long enough, he is sure to get it. Perhaps
that is because he has been a fisherman all his
life, and his father and his grandfather were
fishermen. You know a fisherman without
patience rarely catches anything. Of course
Billy Mink and Little Joe Otter laugh at this
and say that it isn't so, but the truth is they
sometimes go hungry when they wouldn't if
they had a little of the patience of Longlegs.

Now Grandfather Frog is another who is very, very patient. He can sit still the longest time waiting for something to come to him. Indeed, he can sit perfectly still so long, and Longlegs can stand perfectly still so long, that Jerry Muskrat and Billy Mink and Little Joe Otter have had many long disputes as to which of the two can keep still the longest.

"He will make a splendid breakfast," thought Longlegs, as very, very carefully he walked along the edge of the Smiling Pool so as to get right opposite Grandfather Frog. There he stopped and looked very hard at Grandfather Frog. Yes, he certainly must be asleep, for his eyes were closed. Longlegs chuckled to himself right down inside without making a sound, and got ready to wade out so as to get within reach.

Now all the time Grandfather Frog was doing some quiet chuckling himself. You see, he wasn't asleep at all. He was just pretending to be asleep, and all the time he was watching Longlegs out of a corner of one of his big goggly eyes. Very, very slowly and carefully, so as not to make the teeniest, weeniest sound, Longlegs lifted one foot to wade out into the Smiling Pool. Grandfather Frog pretended to yawn and opened his big goggly eyes. Longlegs stood on one foot without moving so much as a feather. Grandfather Frog yawned

again, nodded as if he were too sleepy to keep
awake, and half closed his eyes. Longlegs
waited and waited. Then, little by little, so
slowly that if you had been there you would
hardly have seen him move, he drew his long
neck down until his head rested on his shoulders.

"I guess I must wait until he falls sound
asleep again," said Longlegs to himself.

But Grandfather Frog didn't go to sleep. He
would nod and nod and then, just when Longlegs would make up his mind that this time he
really was asleep, open would pop Grandfather Frog's eyes. So all the long morning Longlegs stood on one foot without moving, watching and waiting and growing hungrier and
hungrier, and all the long morning Grandfather Frog sat on his big green lily-pad, pretending that he was oh, so sleepy, and all the
time having such a comfortable sun-bath and
rest, for very early he had had a good breakfast of foolish green flies.

Over in the bulrushes on the other side of
the Smiling Pool two little scamps in brown
bathing suits waited and watched for the
great fright they had planned for Grandfather
Frog, when they had sent Longlegs to try to
catch him. They were Billy Mink and Little
Joe Otter. At first they laughed to themselves

and nudged each other at the thought of the trick they had played. Then, as nothing happened, they began to grow tired and uneasy. You see they do not possess patience. Finally they gave up in disgust and stole away to find some more exciting sport. Grandfather Frog saw them go and chuckled harder than ever to himself.

V

Grandfather Frog Jumps
Just in Time

BACK AND FORTH over the Green Meadows sailed Whitetail the Marsh Hawk. Like Longlegs the Blue Heron, he was hungry. His sharp eyes peered down among the grasses, looking for something to eat, but some good fairy seemed to have warned the very little people who live there that Whitetail was out hunting. Perhaps it was one of Old Mother West Wind's children, the Merry Little Breezes. You know they are always flitting about trying to do some one a good turn.

They love to dance and romp and play
From dawn to dusk the livelong day,
But more than this they love to find
A chance to do some favor kind.

Anyway, little Mr. Green Snake seemed to know that Whitetail was out hunting and managed to keep out of sight. Danny Meadow Mouse wasn't to be found. Only a few foolish grasshoppers rewarded his patient search, and these only served to make him feel hungrier then ever. But old Whitetail has a great deal of persistence, and in spite of his bad luck, he kept at his hunting, back and forth, back and forth, until he had been all over the Green Meadows. At last he made up his mind that he was wasting time there.

"I'll just have to look over at the Smiling Pool, and if there is nothing there, I'll take a turn or two along the Big River," thought he and straightway started for the Smiling Pool. Long before he reached it, his keen eyes saw Longlegs the Blue Heron standing motionless on the edge of it, and he knew by the looks of Longlegs that he was watching something which he hoped to catch.

"If it's a fish," thought Whitetail, "it will do me no good, for I am no fisherman. But if it's a Frog—well, Frogs are not as good eating as fat Meadow Mice, but they are very filling."

With that he hurried a little faster, and then he saw what Longlegs was watching so intently. It was, as you know, Grandfather Frog sitting on his big green lily-pad. Old Whitetail gave a great sigh of satisfaction. Grandfather Frog certainly would be very filling, very filling, indeed.

Now Longlegs the Blue Heron was so intently watching Grandfather Frog that he saw nothing else, and Grandfather Frog was so busy watching Longlegs that he quite forgot that there might be other dangers. Besides, his back was toward old Whitetail. Of course Whitetail saw this, and it made him almost chuckle aloud. Ever so many times he had tried to catch Grandfather Frog, but always Grandfather Frog had seen him long before he could get near him.

Now, with all his keen sight, old Whitetail had failed to see some one else who was sitting right in plain sight. He had failed because his mind was so full of Grandfather Frog and Longlegs that he forgot to look around, as he usually does. Just skimming the tops of the bulrushes he sailed swiftly out over the Smiling Pool and reached down with his great, cruel claws to clutch Grandfather Frog, who sat there pretending to be asleep, but all the time watching Longlegs and deep down inside chuckling to think how he was fooling Longlegs.

Slap! That was the tail of Jerry Muskrat hitting the water. Grandfather Frog knew what that meant—danger! He didn't know what the danger was, and he didn't wait to find out. There would be time enough for that later. When Jerry Muskrat slapped the water with his tail that way, danger was very near indeed. With a frightened "Chugarum!" Grandfather Frog dived head first into the Smiling Pool, and so close was old Whitetail that the water was splashed right in his face. He clutched frantically with his great claws, but all he got was a piece of the big green lily-pad on which Grandfather Frog had been sitting, and of course this was of no use for an empty stomach.

With a scream of disappointment and anger, he whirled in the air and made straight for Jerry Muskrat. But Jerry just laughed in the most provoking way and ducked under water.

VI

Longlegs and Whitetail Quarrel

"You did!" "I didn't! I didn't!" "You did!"
Such a terrible fuss when Grandfather hid!

Y OU SEE Longlegs the Blue Heron had
stood very patiently on one foot all the
long morning waiting for Grandfather Frog to
go to sleep on his big green lily-pad. He had
felt sure he was to have Grandfather Frog for
his breakfast and lunch, for he had had no
breakfast, and it was now lunch time. He was
so hungry that it seemed to him that the sides
of his stomach certainly would fall in because
there was nothing to hold them up, and then,
without any warning at all, old Whitetail the
Marsh Hawk had glided out across the Smiling Pool with his great claws stretched out to
clutch Grandfather Frog, and Grandfather
Frog had dived into the Smiling Pool with a
great splash just in the very nick of time.

Now is there anything in the world so hard
on the temper as to lose a good meal when
you are very, very, very hungry? Of course
Longlegs didn't really have that good meal,
but he had thought that he was surely going

to have it. So when Grandfather Frog splashed into the Smiling Pool, of course Longlegs lost his temper altogether. His yellow eyes seemed to grow even more yellow.

"You robber! You thief!" he screamed harshly at old Whitetail.

Now old Whitetail was just as hungry as Longlegs, and he had come even nearer to catching Grandfather Frog. He is even quicker tempered than Longlegs. He had whirled like a flash on Jerry Muskrat, but Jerry had just laughed in the most provoking manner and ducked under water. This had made old Whitetail angrier than ever, and then to be called bad names—robber and thief! It was more than any self-respecting Hawk could stand. Yes, Sir, it certainly was! He fairly shook with rage as he turned in the air once more and made straight for Longlegs the Blue Heron.

"I'm no more robber and thief than you are!" he shrieked.

"You frightened away my Frog!" screamed Longlegs.

"I didn't!"

"You did!"

"I didn't! It wasn't your Frog; it was mine!"

"Chugarum!" said Grandfather Frog to Jerry Muskrat, as they peeped out from under some lily-pads. "I didn't know I belonged to any-body. I really didn't. Did you?"

"No," replied Jerry, his eyes sparkling with excitement as he watched Longlegs and Whitetail, "it's news to me."

"You're too lazy to hunt like honest people!" taunted old Whitetail, as he wheeled around Longlegs, watching for a chance to strike with his great, cruel claws.

"I'm too honest to take the food out of other people's mouths!" retorted Longlegs, dancing around so as always to face Whitetail, one of his great, broad wings held in front of him like a shield, and his long, strong bill ready to strike.

Every feather on Whitetail's head was standing erect with rage, and he looked very fierce and terrible. At last he saw a chance, or thought he did, and shot down. But all he got was a feather from that great wing which Long-legs kept in front of him, and before he could get away, that long bill had struck him twice, so that he screamed with pain. So they fought and fought, till the ground was covered with feathers, and they were too tired to fight any longer. Then, slowly and painfully, old White-tail flew away over the Green Meadows, and with torn and ragged wings, Longlegs flew heavily down the Laughing Brook towards the

Big River, and both were sore and stiff and still hungry.

"Dear me! Dear me! What a terrible thing and how useless anger is," said Grandfather Frog, as he climbed back on his big green lily-pad in the warm sunshine.

VII

Grandfather Frog's Big Mouth Gets Him in Trouble

GRANDFATHER FROG has a great big mouth. You know that. Everybody does. His friends of the Smiling Pool, the Laughing Brook, and the Green Meadows have teased Grandfather Frog a great deal about the size of his mouth, but he hasn't minded in the least, not the very least. You see, he learned a long time ago that a big mouth is very handy for catching foolish green flies, especially when two happen to come along together. So he is rather proud of his big mouth, just as he is of his goggly eyes.

But once in a while his big mouth gets him into trouble. It's a way big mouths have. It holds so much that it makes him greedy sometimes. He stuffs it full after his stomach already has all that it can hold, and then of course he can't swallow. Then Grandfather Frog looks very foolish and silly and undignified, and everybody calls him a greedy fellow who is old enough to know better and who ought to be ashamed of himself. Perhaps he is, but he never says so, and he is almost sure to do the same thing over again the first chance he has.

Now it happened that one morning when Grandfather Frog had had a very good breakfast of foolish green flies and really didn't need another single thing to eat, who should come along but Little Joe Otter, who had been down to the Big River fishing. He had eaten all he could hold, and he was taking the rest of his catch to a secret hiding-place up the Laughing Brook.

Now Grandfather Frog is very fond of fish for a change, and when he saw those that Little Joe Otter had, his eyes glistened, and in spite of his full stomach his mouth watered.

"Good morning, Grandfather Frog! Have you had your breakfast yet?" called Little Joe Otter.

Grandfather Frog wanted to say no, but he always tells the truth. "Ye-e-s," he replied.

"I've had my breakfast, such as it was. Why do you ask?"

"Oh, for no reason in particular. I just thought that if you hadn't, you might like a fish. But as long as you have breakfasted, of course you don't want one," said Little Joe, his bright eyes beginning to twinkle. He held the fish out so that Grandfather Frog could see just how plump and nice they were.

"Chugarum!" exclaimed Grandfather Frog. "Those certainly are very nice fish, very nice fish indeed. It is very nice of you to think of a poor old fellow like me, and I—er—well, I might find room for just a little teeny, weeny one, if you can spare it."

Little Joe Otter knows all about Grandfather Frog's greediness. He looked at Grandfather Frog's white and yellow waistcoat and saw how it was already stuffed full to bursting. The twinkle in his eyes grew more mischievous than ever as he said: "Of course I can. But I wouldn't think of giving such an old friend a teeny, weeny one."

With that, Little Joe picked out the biggest fish he had and tossed it over to Grandfather Frog. It landed close by his nose with a great splash, and it was almost half as big as Grandfather Frog himself. It was plump and looked so tempting that Grandfather Frog forgot all about his full stomach. He even forgot to be polite and thank Little Joe Otter. He just opened his great mouth and seized the fish. Yes, Sir, that is just what he did. Almost before you could wink an eye, the fish had started down Grandfather Frog's throat head first.

Now you know Grandfather Frog has no teeth, and so he cannot bite things in two. He has to swallow them whole. That is just what he started to do with the fish. It went all right until the head reached his stomach. But you can't put anything more into a thing already full, and Grandfather Frog's stomach was packed as full as it could be of foolish green flies. There the fish stuck, and gulp and swallow as hard as he could, Grandfather Frog couldn't make that fish go a bit farther. Then he tried to get it out again, but it had gone so far down his throat that he couldn't get it back. Grandfather Frog began to choke.

VIII

Spotty the Turtle Plays Doctor

Greed's a dreadful thing to see,
As everybody will agree.

AT FIRST Little Joe Otter, sitting on the bank of the Smiling Pool, laughed himself almost sick as he watched Grandfather Frog trying to swallow a fish almost as big as himself, when his white and yellow waistcoat was already stuffed so full of foolish green flies that there wasn't room for anything more. Such greed would have been disgusting, if it hadn't been so very, very funny. At least, it was funny at first, for the fish had stuck, with the tail hanging out of Grandfather Frog's big mouth. Grandfather Frog hitched this way and hitched that way on his big green lily-pad, trying his best to swallow. Twice he tumbled off with a splash into the Smiling Pool. Each time he scrambled back again and rolled his great goggly eyes in silent appeal to Little Joe Otter to come to his aid.

But Little Joe was laughing so that he had to hold his sides, and he didn't understand that Grandfather Frog really was in trouble.

Billy Mink and Jerry Muskrat came along, and
as soon as they saw Grandfather Frog, they
began to laugh, too. They just laughed and
laughed and laughed until the tears came.
They rolled over and over on the bank and
kicked their heels from sheer enjoyment. It
was the funniest thing they had seen for a
long, long time.

"Did you ever see such greed?" gasped Billy
Mink.

"Why don't you pull it out and start over
again?" shouted Little Joe Otter.

Now this is just what Grandfather Frog was
trying to do. At least, he was trying to pull the
fish out. He hadn't the least desire in the
world to try swallowing it again. In fact, he
felt just then as if he never, never wanted to
see another fish so long as he lived. But
Grandfather Frog's hands are not made for
grasping slippery things, and the tail of a fish
is very slippery indeed. He tried first with one
hand, then with the other, and at last with
both. It was of no use at all. He just couldn't
budge that fish. He couldn't cough it up,
because it had gone too far down for that. The
more he clawed at that waving tail with his
hands, the funnier he looked, and the harder
Little Joe Otter and Billy Mink and Jerry
Muskrat laughed. They made such a noise that

As soon as they saw Grandfather Frog, they began
to laugh, too. *Page 27.*

Spotty the Turtle, who had been taking a sun-bath on the end of an old log, slipped into the water and started to see what it was all about.

Now Spotty the Turtle is very, very slow on land, but he is a good swimmer. He hurried now because he didn't want to miss the fun. At first he didn't see Grandfather Frog.

"What's the joke?" he asked.

Little Joe Otter simply pointed to Grandfather Frog. Little Joe had laughed so much that he couldn't even speak. Spotty looked over to the big green lily-pad and started to laugh too. Then he saw great tears rolling down from Grandfather Frog's eyes and heard little choky sounds. He stopped laughing and started for Grandfather Frog as fast as he could swim. He climbed right up on the big green lily-pad, and reaching out, grabbed the end of the fish tail in his beak-like mouth. Then Spotty the Turtle settled back and pulled, and Grandfather Frog settled back and pulled. Splash! Grandfather Frog had fallen backward into the Smiling Pool on one side of the big green lily-pad. Splash! Spotty the Turtle had fallen backward into the Smiling Pool on the opposite side of the big green lily-pad. And the fish which had caused all the trouble lay floating on the water.

"Thank you! Thank you!" gasped Grandfather Frog, as he feebly crawled back on the lily-pad. "A minute more, and I would have choked to death."

"Don't mention it," replied Spotty the Turtle.

"I never, never will," promised Grandfather Frog.

IX

Old Mr. Toad Visits Grandfather Frog

GRANDFATHER FROG and old Mr. Toad are cousins. Of course you know that without being told. Everybody does. But not everybody knows that they were born in the same place. They were. Yes, Sir, they were. They were born in the Smiling Pool. Both had long tails and for a while no legs, and they played and swam together without ever going on shore. In fact, when they were babies, they couldn't live out of the water. And people who saw them didn't know the difference between them and called them by the same names — tadpoles or pollywogs. But when they grew old enough to have legs and get along without tails, they parted company.

You see, it was this way: Grandfather Frog (of course he wasn't grandfather then) loved the Smiling Pool so well that he couldn't think of leaving it. He heard all about the Great World and what a wonderful place it was, but he couldn't and wouldn't believe that there could be any nicer place than the Smiling Pool, and so he made up his mind that he would live there always.

But Mr. Toad could hardly wait to get rid of his tail before turning his back on the Smiling Pool and starting out to see the Great World. Nothing that Grandfather Frog could say would stop him, and away Mr. Toad went, when he was so small that he could hide under a clover leaf. Grandfather Frog didn't expect ever to see him again. But he did, though it wasn't for a long, long time. And when he did come back, he had grown so that Grandfather Frog hardly knew him at first. And right then and there began a dispute which they have kept up ever since: whether it was best to go out into the Great World or remain in the home of childhood. Each was sure that what he had done was best, and each is sure of it to this day.

So whenever old Mr. Toad visits Grandfather Frog, as he does every once in a while, they are sure to argue and argue on this same old subject. It was so on the day that Grand-

father Frog had so nearly choked to death.
Old Mr. Toad had heard about it from one of
the Merry Little Breezes of Old Mother West
Wind and right away had started for the Smiling Pool to pay his respects to Grandfather
Frog, and to tell him how glad he was that
Spotty the Turtle had come along just in time
to pull the fish out of Grandfather Frog's
throat.

Now all day long Grandfather Frog had had
to listen to unpleasant remarks about his
greediness. It was such a splendid chance to
tease him that everybody around the Smiling
Pool took advantage of it. Grandfather Frog
took it good-naturedly at first, but after a
while it made him cross, and by the time his
cousin, old Mr. Toad, arrived, he was sulky
and just grunted when Mr. Toad told him how
glad he was to find Grandfather Frog quite
recovered.

Old Mr. Toad pretended not to notice how
out of sorts Grandfather Frog was but kept
right on talking.

"If you had been out in the Great World as
much as I have been, you would have known
that Little Joe Otter wasn't giving you that fish
for nothing," said he.

Grandfather Frog swelled right out with
anger. "Chugarum!" he exclaimed in his deep-
est, gruffest voice. "Chugarum! Go back to

your Great World and learn to mind your own affairs, Mr. Toad."

Right away old Mr. Toad began to swell with anger too. For a whole minute he glared at Grandfather Frog, so indignant he couldn't find his tongue. When he did find it, he said some very unpleasant things, and right away they began to dispute.

"What good are you to anybody but yourself, never seeing anything of the Great World and not knowing anything about what is going on or what other people are doing?" asked old Mr. Toad.

"I'm minding my own affairs and not meddling with things that don't concern me, as seems to be the way out in the Great World you are so fond of talking about," retorted Grandfather Frog. "Wise people know enough to be content with what they have. You've been out in the Great World ever since you could hop, and what good has it done you? Tell me that! You haven't even a decent suit of clothes to your back." Grandfather Frog patted his white and yellow waistcoat as he spoke and looked admiringly at the reflection of his handsome green coat in the Smiling Pool.

Old Mr. Toad's eyes snapped, for you know his suit is very plain and rough.

"People who do honest work for their living

have no time to sit about in fine clothes admiring themselves," he replied sharply. "I've learned this much out in the Great World, that lazy people come to no good end, and I know enough not to choke myself to death."

Grandfather Frog almost choked again, he was so angry. You see old Mr. Toad's remarks were very personal, and nobody likes personal remarks when they are unpleasant, especially if they happen to be true. Grandfather Frog was trying his best to think of something sharp to say in reply, when Mr. Redwing, sitting in the top of the big hickory-tree, shouted: "Here comes Farmer Brown's boy!"

Grandfather Frog forgot his anger and began to look anxious. He moved about uneasily on his big green lily-pad and got ready to dive into the Smiling Pool, for he was afraid that Farmer Brown's boy had a pocketful of stones as he usually did have when he came over to the Smiling Pool.

Old Mr. Toad didn't look troubled the least bit. He didn't even look around for a hiding-place. He just sat still and grinned.

"You'd better watch out, or you'll never visit the Smiling Pool again," called Grandfather Frog.

"Oh," replied old Mr. Toad, "I'm not afraid. Farmer Brown's boy is a friend of mine. I help him in his garden. How to make friends is one of the things the Great World has taught me."

"Chugarum!" said Grandfather Frog. "I'd have you to know that—"

But what it was that he was to know old Mr. Toad never found out, for just then Grandfather Frog caught sight of Farmer Brown's boy and without waiting even to say good-by he dived into the Smiling Pool.

X

Grandfather Frog Starts Out to See the Great World

GRANDFATHER FROG looked very solemn as he sat on his big green lily-pad in the Smiling Pool. He looked very much as if he had something on his mind. A foolish green fly actually brushed Grandfather Frog's nose and he didn't even notice it. The fact is he did have something on his mind. It had been there ever since his cousin, old Mr. Toad, had called the day before and they had quarreled as usual over the question whether it was best never to leave home or to go out into the Great World.

Right in the midst of their quarrel along had

come Farmer Brown's boy. Now Grandfather
Frog is afraid of Farmer Brown's boy, so
when he appeared, Grandfather Frog stopped
arguing with old Mr. Toad and with a great
splash dived into the Smiling Pool and hid
under a lily-pad. There he stayed and watched
his cousin, old Mr. Toad, grinning in the most
provoking way, for he wasn't afraid of Farmer
Brown's boy. In fact, he had boasted that they
were friends. Grandfather Frog had thought
that this was just an idle boast, but when he
saw Farmer Brown's boy tickle old Mr. Toad
under his chin with a straw, while Mr. Toad
sat perfectly still and seemed to enjoy it, he
knew that it was true.

Grandfather Frog had not come out of his
hiding-place until after old Mr. Toad had gone
back across the Green Meadows and Farmer
Brown's boy had gone home for his supper.
Then Grandfather Frog had climbed back on
his big green lily-pad and had sat there half
the night without once leading the chorus of
the Smiling Pool with his great deep bass
voice as he usually did. He was thinking,
thinking very hard. And now, this bright, sunshiny morning, he was still thinking.

The fact is Grandfather Frog was beginning
to wonder if perhaps, after all, Mr. Toad was
right. If the Great World had taught him how

to make friends with Farmer Brown's boy,
there really must be some things worth learn-
ing there. Not for the world would Grandfather Frog have admitted to old Mr. Toad or
to any one else that there was anything for
him to learn, for you know he is very old and
by his friends is accounted very wise. But
right down in his heart he was beginning to
think that perhaps there were some things
which he couldn't learn in the Smiling Pool.
So he sat and thought and thought. Suddenly
he made up his mind.

"Chugarum!" said he. "I'll do it!"

"Do what?" asked Jerry Muskrat, who happened to be swimming past.

"I'll go out and see for myself what this
Great World my cousin, old Mr. Toad, is so
fond of talking about is like," replied Grandfather Frog.

"Don't you do it," advised Jerry Muskrat.
"Don't you do anything so foolish as that.
You're too old, much too old, Grandfather
Frog, to go out into the Great World."

Now few old people like to be told that they
are too old to do what they please, and Grandfather Frog is no different from others. "You
just mind your own affairs, Jerry Muskrat," he
retorted sharply. "I guess I know what is best
for me without being told. If my cousin, old

Mr. Toad, can take care of himself out in the Great World, I can. He isn't half so spry as I am. I'm going, and that is all there is about it!"

With that Grandfather Frog dived into the Smiling Pool, swam across to a place where the bank was low, and without once looking back started across the Green Meadows to see the Great World.

XI

Grandfather Frog Is Stubborn

"Fee, fi, fe, fum!
Chug, chug, chugarum!"

GRANDFATHER actually had started out to see the Great World. Yes, Sir, he had turned his back on the Smiling Pool, and nothing that Jerry Muskrat could say made the least bit of difference. Grandfather Frog had made up his mind, and when he does that, it is just a waste of time and breath for any one to try to make him change it. You see Grandfather Frog is stubborn. Yes, that is just the word—stubborn. He would see for himself what this Great World was that his cousin, old

Mr. Toad, talked so much about and said was so much better than the Smiling Pool where Grandfather Frog had spent his whole life.

"If old Mr. Toad can take care of himself, I can take care of myself out in the Great World," said Grandfather Frog to himself as, with great jumps, he started out on to the Green Meadows. "I guess he isn't any smarter than I am! He isn't half so spry as I am, and I can jump three times as far as he can. I'll see for myself what this Great World is like, and then I'll go back to the Smiling Pool and stay there the rest of my life. Chugarum, how warm it is!"

It was warm. Jolly, round, bright Mr. Sun was smiling his broadest and pouring his warmest rays down on the Green Meadows. The Merry Little Breezes of Old Mother West Wind were taking a nap. You see, they had played so hard early in the morning that they were tired. So there was nobody and nothing to cool Grandfather Frog, and he just grew warmer and warmer with every jump. He began to grow thirsty, and how he did long for a plunge in the dear, cool Smiling Pool! But he was stubborn. He wouldn't turn back, no matter how uncomfortable he felt. He *would* see the Great World if it killed him. So he kept right on, jump, jump, jump, jump.

Grandfather Frog had been up the Laughing Brook and down the Laughing Brook, where he could swim when he grew tired of traveling on the bank, and where he could cool off whenever he became too warm, but never before had he been very far away from water, and he found this a very different matter. At first he had made great jumps, for that is what his long legs were given him for; but the long grass bothered him, and after a little the jumps grew shorter and shorter and shorter, and with every jump he puffed and puffed and presently began to grunt. You see he never before had made more than a few jumps at a time without resting, and his legs grew tired in a very little while.

Now if Grandfather Frog had known as much about the Green Meadows as the little people who live there all the time do, he would have taken the Lone Little Path, where the going was easy. But he didn't. He just started right out without knowing where he was going, and of course the way was hard, very hard indeed. The grass was so tall that he couldn't see over it, and the ground was so rough that it hurt his tender feet, which were used to the soft, mossy bank of the Smiling Pool. He had gone only a little way before he wished with all his might that he had never thought of seeing the Great World. But he had said that he was going to and he would, so he kept right on—jump, jump, rest, jump, jump, jump, rest, jump, and then a long rest.

It was during one of these rests that he heard footsteps, and then a dreadful sound that made cold chills run all over him. Sniff, sniff, sniff! It was coming nearer. Grandfather Frog flattened himself down as close to the ground as he could get. But it was of no use, no use at all. The sniffing came nearer and nearer, and then right over him stood Bowser the Hound! Bowser looked just as surprised as he felt. He put out one paw and turned Grandfather Frog over on his back. Grandfather Frog struggled to his feet and made two frightened jumps.

"Bow, wow!" cried Bowser and rolled him over again. Bowser thought it great fun, but Grandfather Frog thought that his last day had come.

XII

Grandfather Frog Keeps On

Grandfather Frog is old and wise,
   But even age is foolish.
I'm sure you'll all agree with me
   His stubbornness was mulish.

THAT HIS very last day had come Grandfather Frog was sure. He didn't have the least doubt about it. Here he was at the mercy of Bowser the Hound out on the Green Meadows far from the dear, safe Smiling Pool. Every time he moved, Bowser flipped him over on his back and danced around him, barking with joy. Every minute Grandfather Frog expected to feel Bowser's terrible teeth, and he grew cold at the thought. When he found that he couldn't get away, he just lay still. He was too tired and frightened to do much of anything else, anyway.

Now when he lay still, he spoiled Bowser's fun, for it was seeing him jump and kick his long legs that tickled Bowser so. Bowser tossed him up in the air two or three times, but Grandfather Frog simply lay where he fell without moving.

"Bow, wow, wow!" cried Bowser, in his great deep voice. Grandfather Frog didn't so much as blink his great goggly eyes. Bowser sniffed him all over.

"I guess I've frightened him to death," said Bowser, talking to himself. "I didn't mean to do that. I just wanted to have some fun with him." With that, Bowser took one more sniff and then trotted off to try to find something more exciting. You see, he hadn't had the least intention in the world of really hurting Grandfather Frog.

Grandfather Frog kept perfectly still until he was sure that Bowser was nowhere near. Then he gave a great sigh of relief and crawled under a big mullein leaf to rest, and think things over.

"Chugarum, that was a terrible experience; it was, indeed!" said he to himself, shivering at the very thought of what he had been through. "Nothing like that ever happened to me in the Smiling Pool. I've always said that the Smiling Pool is a better place in which to live than is the Great World, and now I know it. The question is, what had I best do now?"

Now right down in his heart Grandfather Frog knew the answer. Of course the best thing to do was to go straight back to the Smiling Pool as fast as he could. But Grand-

father Frog is stubborn. Yes, Sir, he certainly
is stubborn. And stubbornness is often just
another name for foolishness. He had told
Jerry Muskrat that he was going out to see the
Great World. Now if he went back, Jerry
would laugh at him.

"I won't!" said Grandfather Frog.

"What won't you do?" asked a voice so
close to him that Grandfather Frog made a
long jump before he thought. You see, at the
Smiling Pool he always jumped at the least
hint of danger, and because one jump always
took him into the water, he was always safe.
But there was no water here, and that jump
took him right out where anybody passing
could see him. Then he turned around to see
who had startled him so. It was Danny
Meadow Mouse.

"I won't go back to the Smiling Pool until
I have seen the Great World," replied Grandfather Frog gruffly.

"You won't see much of the Great World if
you jump like that every time you get a scare,"
said Danny, shaking his head. "No, Sir, you
won't see much of the Great World, because
one of these times you'll jump right into the
claws of old Whitetail the Marsh Hawk, or his
cousin Redtail, or Reddy Fox. You take my
advice, Grandfather Frog, and go straight

"You won't see much of the Great World if you jump like that every time you get a scare," said Danny. *Page 44.*

back to the Smiling Pool. You don't know enough about the Great World to take care of yourself."

But Grandfather Frog was set in his ways, and nothing that Danny Meadow Mouse could say changed his mind in the least. "I started out to see the Great World, and I'm going to keep right on," said he.

"All right," said Danny at last. "If you will, I suppose you will. I'll go a little way with you just to get you started right."

"Thank you," replied Grandfather Frog. "Let's start right away."

XIII

Danny Meadow Mouse
Feels Responsible

RESPONSIBLE is a great big word. But it is just as big in its meaning as it is in its looks, and that is the way words should be, I think, don't you? Anyway, re-spon-sible is the way Danny Meadow Mouse felt when he found Grandfather Frog out on the Green Meadows so far from the Smiling Pool and so stubborn that he would keep on to see the Great World instead of going back to his big green lily-pad in the Smiling Pool, where he could take care of himself. You remember Peter Rabbit felt re-spon-sible when he brought little Miss Fuzzytail down from the Old Pasture to the dear Old Briar-patch. He felt that it was his business to see to it that no harm came to her, and that is just the way Danny Meadow Mouse felt about Grandfather Frog.

You see, Danny knew that if Grandfather Frog was going to jump like that every time he was frightened, he wouldn't get very far in the Great World. It might be the right thing to do in the Smiling Pool, where the friendly water would hide him from his enemies, but it was just the wrong thing to do on the Green Meadows or in the Green Forest. Danny had learned, when a very tiny fellow, that there the only safe thing to do when danger was near was to sit perfectly still and hardly breathe.

Now Danny Meadow Mouse is fond of Grandfather Frog, and he couldn't bear to think that something dreadful might happen to him. So when he found that he couldn't get Grandfather Frog to go back to the Smiling Pool, he made up his mind that he just *had* to

go along with Grandfather Frog to try to keep
him out of danger. Yes, Sir, he just *had* to do
it. He felt re-spon-sible for Grandfather Frog's
safety. So here they were, Danny Meadow
Mouse running ahead, anxious and worried
and watching sharply for signs of danger, and
Grandfather Frog puffing along behind, bound
to see the Great World which his cousin, old
Mr. Toad, said was a better place to live in
than the Smiling Pool.

Now Danny has a great many private little
paths under the grass all over the Green
Meadows, and along these he can scamper
ever so fast without once showing himself to
those who may be looking for him. Of course
he started to take Grandfather Frog along one
of these little paths. But Grandfather Frog
doesn't walk or run; he jumps. There wasn't
room in Danny's little paths for jumping, as
they soon found out. Grandfather Frog simply
couldn't follow Danny along those little paths.
Danny sat down to think, and puckered his
brows anxiously. He was more worried than
ever. It was very clear that Grandfather Frog
would have to travel out in the open, where
there was room for him to jump, and where
also he would be right out in plain sight of all
who happened along. Once more Danny urged
him to go back to the Smiling Pool, but he

might just as well have talked to a stick or a stone. Grandfather Frog had started out to see the Great World, and he was going to see it.

Danny sighed. "If you will, you will, I suppose," said he, "and I guess the only place you can travel in any comfort is the Lone Little Path. It is dangerous, very dangerous, but I guess you will have to do it."

"Chugarum!" replied Grandfather Frog, "I'm not afraid. You show me the Lone Little Path and then go about your business, Danny Meadow Mouse."

So Danny led the way to the Lone Little Path, and Grandfather Frog sighed with relief, for here he could jump without getting all tangled up in long grass and without hurting his tender feet on sharp stubble where the grass had been cut. But Danny felt more worried than ever. He wouldn't leave Grandfather Frog because, you know, he felt re-spon-sible for him, and at the same time he was terribly afraid, for he felt sure that some of their enemies would see them. He wanted to go back, but he kept right on, and that shows just what a brave little fellow Danny Meadow Mouse was.

XIV

Grandfather Frog Has a Strange Ride

A thousand things may happen to,
Ten thousand things befall,
The traveler who careless is,
Or thinks he knows it all.

GRANDFATHER FROG, jumping along behind Danny Meadow Mouse up the Lone Little Path, was beginning to think that Danny was the most timid and easiest frightened of all the little meadow people of his acquaintance. Danny kept as much under the grass that overhung the Lone Little Path as he could. When there were perfectly bare places, Danny looked this way and looked that way anxiously and then scampered across as fast as he could make his little legs go. When he was safely across, he would wait for Grandfather Frog. If a shadow passed over the grass, Danny would duck under the nearest leaf and hold his breath.

"Foolish!" muttered Grandfather Frog. "Foolish, foolish to be so afraid! Now, I'm not afraid until I see something to be afraid of.

Time enough then. What's the good of looking for trouble all the time? Now, here I am out in the Great World, and I'm not afraid. And here's Danny Meadow Mouse, who has lived here all his life, acting as if he expected something dreadful to happen any minute. Pooh! How very, very foolish!"

Now Grandfather Frog is old and in the Smiling Pool he is accounted very, very wise. But the wisest sometimes become foolish when they think that they know all there is to know. It was so with Grandfather Frog. It was he who was foolish and not Danny Meadow Mouse. You see Danny knew all the dangers on the Green Meadows, and how many sharp eyes were all the time watching for him. He had long ago learned that the only way to feel safe was to feel afraid. You see, then he was watching for danger every minute, and so he wasn't likely to be surprised by his hungry enemies.

So while Grandfather Frog was looking down on Danny for being so timid, Danny was really doing the wisest thing. More than that, he was really very, very brave. He was showing Grandfather Frog the way up the Lone Little Path to see the Great World, when he himself would never, never have thought of traveling anywhere but along his own secret little paths, just because Grandfather Frog couldn't jump anywhere excepting where the way was fairly clear, as in the Lone Little Path, and Danny was afraid that unless Grandfather Frog had some one with him to watch out for him, he would surely come to a sad end.

The farther they went with nothing happening, the more foolish Danny's timid way of running and hiding seemed to Grandfather Frog, and he was just about to tell Danny just what he thought, when Danny dived into the long grass and warned Grandfather Frog to do the same. But Grandfather Frog didn't.

"Chugarum!" said he, "I don't see anything to be afraid of, and I'm not going to hide until I do."

So he sat still right where he was, in the middle of the Lone Little Path, looking this way and that way, and seeing nothing to be afraid of. And just then around a turn in the Lone Little Path came—who do you think? Why Farmer Brown's boy! He saw Grandfather Frog and with a whoop of joy he sprang for him. Grandfather Frog gave a frightened croak and jumped, but he was too late. Before he could jump again Farmer Brown's boy had him by his long hind-legs.

"Ha, ha!" shouted Farmer Brown's boy, "I

believe this is the very old chap I have tried so often to catch in the Smiling Pool. These legs of yours will be mighty fine eating, Mr. Frog. They will, indeed."

With that he tied Grandfather Frog's legs together and went on his way across the Green Meadows with poor old Grandfather Frog dangling from the end of a string. It was a strange ride and a most uncomfortable one, and with all his might Grandfather Frog wished he had never thought of going out into the Great World.

XV

Grandfather Frog
Gives Up Hope

WITH HIS LEGS tied together, hanging head down from the end of a string, Grandfather Frog was being carried he knew not where by Farmer Brown's boy. It was dreadful. Half-way across the Green Meadows the Merry Little Breezes of Old Mother West Wind came dancing along. At first they didn't see Grandfather Frog, but presently one of

them, rushing up to tease Farmer Brown's boy
by blowing off his hat, caught sight of Grandfather Frog.

Now the Merry Little Breezes are great
friends of Grandfather Frog. Many, many
times they have blown foolish green flies over
to him as he sat on his big green lily-pad, and
they are very fond of him. So when this one
caught sight of him in such a dreadful posi-
tion, he forgot all about teasing Farmer
Brown's boy. He raced away to tell the other
Merry Little Breezes. For a minute they were
perfectly still. They forgot all about being
merry.

"It's awful, just perfectly awful!" cried one.

"We must do something to help Grandfather
Frog!" cried another.

"Of course we must," said a third.

"But what can we do?" asked a fourth.

Nobody replied. They just thought and
thought and thought. Finally the first one
spoke. "We might try to comfort him a little,"
said he.

"Of course we will do that!" they shouted
all together.

"And if we throw dust in the face of Farmer
Brown's boy and steal his hat, perhaps he will
put Grandfather Frog down," continued the
Merry Little Breeze.

"The very thing!" the others cried, dancing about with excitement.

"Then we can rush about and tell all Grandfather Frog's friends what has happened to him and where he is. Perhaps some of them can help us," the Little Breeze continued.

They wasted no more time talking, but raced after Farmer Brown's boy as fast as they could go. One of them, who was faster than the others, ran ahead and whispered in Grandfather Frog's ear that they were coming to help him. But poor old Grandfather Frog couldn't be comforted. He couldn't see what there was that the Merry Little Breezes could do. His legs smarted where the string cut into the skin, and his head ached, for you know he was hanging head down. No, Sir, Grandfather Frog couldn't be comforted. He was in a terrible fix, and he couldn't see any way out of it. He hadn't the least bit of hope left. And all the time Farmer Brown's boy was trudging along, whistling merrily. You see, it didn't occur to him to think how Grandfather Frog must be suffering and how terribly frightened he must be. He wasn't cruel. No, indeed, Farmer Brown's boy wasn't cruel. That is, he didn't mean to be cruel. He was just thoughtless, like a great many other boys, and girls too.

So he went whistling on his way until he

reached the Long Lane leading from the Green Meadows up to Farmer Brown's door-yard. No sooner was he in the Long Lane than something happened. A great cloud of dust and leaves and tiny sticks was dashed in his face and nearly choked him. Dirt got in his eyes. His hat was snatched from his head and went sailing over into the garden. He dropped Grandfather Frog and felt for his handker-chief to wipe the dirt from his eyes.

"Phew!" exclaimed Farmer Brown's boy, as he started after his hat. "It's funny where that wind came from so suddenly!"

But you know and I know that it was the Merry Little Breezes working together who made up that sudden wind. And Grandfather Frog ought to have known it too, but he didn't. You see the dust had got in his nose and eyes just as it had in those of Farmer Brown's boy, and he was so frightened and confused that he couldn't think. So he lay just where Farmer Brown's boy dropped him, and he didn't have any more hope than before.

XVI

The Merry Little Breezes
Work Hard

THE MERRY LITTLE BREEZES almost shouted aloud with delight when they saw Farmer Brown's boy drop Grandfather Frog to feel for his handkerchief and wipe out the dust which they had thrown in his eyes. Then he had to climb the fence and chase his hat through the garden. They would let him almost get his hands on it and then, just as he thought that he surely had it, they would snatch it away. It was great fun for the Merry Little Breezes. But they were not doing it for fun. No, indeed, they were not doing it for fun! They were doing it to lead Farmer Brown's boy away from Grandfather Frog.

Just as soon as they dared, they dropped the hat and then separated and rushed away in all directions across the Green Meadows, over to the Green Forest, and down to the Smiling Pool. What were they going for? Why, to hunt for some of Grandfather Frog's friends and ask their help. You see, the Merry Little Breezes could make Farmer Brown's boy drop Grandfather Frog, but they couldn't untie a knot or cut a string, and this is just what had got to be done to set Grandfather Frog free, for his hind-legs were tied together. So now they were looking for some one with sharp teeth, who thought enough of Grandfather Frog to come and help him.

One thought of Striped Chipmunk and started for the old stone wall to look for him. Another went in search of Danny Meadow Mouse. A third headed for the dear Old Briarpatch after Peter Rabbit. A fourth remembered Jimmy Skunk and how he had once set Blacky the Crow free from a snare. A fifth remembered what sharp teeth Happy Jack Squirrel has and hurried over to the Green Forest to look for him. A sixth started straight for the Smiling Pool to tell Jerry Muskrat. And every one of them raced as fast as he could.

All this time Grandfather Frog was without hope. Yes, Sir, poor old Grandfather Frog was wholly in despair. You see, he didn't know what the Merry Little Breezes were trying to do, and he was so frightened and confused that he couldn't think. When Farmer Brown's boy dropped him, he lay right where he fell for a few minutes. Then, right close at hand, he saw an old board. Without really thinking, he tried to get to it, for there looked as if there might be room for him to hide under it. It was hard work, for you know his long hind-legs, which he uses for jumping, were tied together. The best he could do was to crawl and wriggle and pull himself along. Just as Farmer Brown's boy started to climb the fence back into the Long Lane, his hat in his hand, Grandfather Frog reached the old board and crawled under it.

Now when the Merry Little Breezes had thrown the dust in Farmer Brown's boy's face and snatched his hat, he had dropped Grand-father Frog in such a hurry that he didn't notice just where he did drop him, so now he didn't know the exact place to look for him. But he knew pretty near, and he hadn't the least doubt but that he would find him. He had just started to look when the dinner horn sounded. Farmer Brown's boy hesitated. He was hungry. If he was late, he might lose his dinner. He could come back later to look for Grandfather Frog, for with his legs tied Grandfather Frog couldn't get far. So, with a last look to make sure of the place, Farmer Brown's boy started for the house.

If the Merry Little Breezes had known this, they would have felt ever so much better. But they didn't. So they hurried as fast as ever they could to find Grandfather Frog's friends

and worked until they were almost too tired
to move, for it seemed as if every single one
of Grandfather Frog's friends had taken that
particular day to go away from home. So
while Farmer Brown's boy ate his dinner, and
Grandfather Frog lay hiding under the old
board in the Long Lane, the Merry Little
Breezes did their best to find help for him.

XVII
Striped Chipmunk Cuts
the String

"Hippy hop! Flippy flop! All on a summer day
My mother turned me from the house and
　　sent me out to play!"

STRIPED CHIPMUNK knew perfectly well
that that was just nonsense, but Striped
Chipmunk learned a long time ago that when
you are just bubbling right over with good
feeling, there is fun in saying and doing foolish things, and that is just how he was feeling.
So he ran along the old rail fence on one side
of the Long Lane, saying foolish things and
cutting up foolish capers just because he felt

so good, and all the time seeing all that those bright little eyes of his could take in.

Now Striped Chipmunk and the Merry Little Breezes of Old Mother West Wind are great friends, very great friends, indeed. Almost every morning they have a grand frolic together. But this morning the Merry Little Breezes hadn't come over to the old stone wall where Striped Chipmunk makes his home. Anyway, they hadn't come at the usual time. Striped Chipmunk had waited a little while and then, because he was feeling so good, he had decided to take a run down the Long Lane to see if anything new had happened there. That is how it happened that when one of the Merry Little Breezes did go to look for him, and was terribly anxious to ask him to come to the help of Grandfather Frog, he was nowhere to be found.

But Striped Chipmunk didn't know anything about that. He scampered along the top rails of the old fence, jumped up on top of a post, and sat up to wash his face and hands, for Striped Chipmunk is very neat and cannot bear to be the least bit dirty. He looked up and winked at Ol' Mistah Buzzard, sailing round and round way, way up in the blue, blue sky. He chased his own tail round and round until he nearly fell off of the post. He made a wry face in the direction of Redtail the Hawk, whom he could see sitting in the top of a tall tree way over on the Green Meadows. He scolded Bowser the Hound, who happened to come trotting up the Long Lane, and didn't stop scolding until Bowser was out of sight. Then he kicked up his heels and whisked along the old fence again.

Half-way across a shaky old rail, he suddenly stopped. His bright eyes had seen something that filled him with curiosity, quite as much curiosity as Peter Rabbit would have had. It was a piece of string. Yes, Sir, it was a piece of string. Now Striped Chipmunk often had found pieces of string, so there was nothing particularly interesting in the string itself. What did interest him and make him very curious was the fact that this piece of string kept moving. Every few seconds it gave a little jerk. Whoever heard of a piece of string moving all by itself? Certainly Striped Chipmunk never had. He couldn't understand it.

For a few minutes he watched it from the top rail of the old fence. Then he scurried down to the ground and, a few steps at a time, stopping to watch sharply between each little run, he drew nearer and nearer to that queer acting string. It gave him a funny feeling inside to see a string acting like that, so he was very careful not to get too near. He looked at it from one side, then ran around and looked at it from the other side. At last he got where he could see that one end of the string was under an old board, and then he began to understand. Of course there was somebody hiding under that old board and jerking the string.

Striped Chipmunk sat down and scratched his head thoughtfully. Whoever was pulling that string couldn't be very big, or they would never have been able to crawl under that old board, therefore he needn't be afraid. A gleam of mischief twinkled in Striped Chipmunk's eyes. He seized the other end of the string and began to pull. Such a jerking and yanking as began right away! But he held on and pulled harder. Then out from under the old board appeared the queer webbed feet of Grandfather Frog tied together. Striped Chipmunk was so surprised that he let go of the string and nearly fell over backward.

"Why, Grandfather Frog, what under the sun are you doing here?" he shouted.

When Striped Chipmunk let go of the string, Grandfather Frog promptly drew his feet back under the old board, but when he heard Striped Chipmunk's voice, he slowly and painfully crawled out. He told how he had been

He seized the other end of the string and began to
pull. *Page 63.*

caught and tied by Farmer Brown's boy and
finally dropped near the old board. He told
how terribly frightened he was, and how sore
his legs were. Striped Chipmunk didn't wait
for him to finish. In a flash he was at work
with his sharp teeth and had cut the cruel
string before Grandfather Frog had finished
his story.

XVIII

Grandfather Frog Hurries Away

WHEN STRIPED CHIPMUNK cut the
string that bound the long legs of
Grandfather Frog together, Grandfather Frog
was so relieved that he hardly knew what to
do. Of course he thanked Striped Chipmunk
over and over again. Striped Chipmunk said
that it was nothing, just nothing at all, and
that he was very glad indeed to help Grandfather Frog.

"We folks who live out in the Great World
have to help one another," said Striped Chipmunk, "because we never know when we may
need help ourselves. Now you take my advice,

Grandfather Frog, and go back to the Smiling Pool as fast as you can. The Great World is no place for an old fellow like you, because you don't know how to take care of yourself."

Now when he said that, Striped Chipmunk made a great mistake. Old people never like to be told that they are old or that they do not know all there is to know. Grandfather Frog straightened up and tried to look very dignified.

"Chugarum!" said he, "I'd have you to know, Striped Chipmunk, that people were coming to me for advice before you were born. It was just an accident that Farmer Brown's boy caught me, and I'd like to see him do it again. Yes, Sir, I'd like to see him do it again!"

Dear me, dear me! Grandfather Frog was boasting. If he had been safe at home in the Smiling Pool, there might have been some excuse for boasting, but way over here in the Long Lane, not even knowing the way back to the Smiling Pool, it was foolish, very foolish indeed. No one knew that better than Striped Chipmunk, but he has a great deal of respect for Grandfather Frog, and he knew too that Grandfather Frog was feeling very much out of sorts and very much mortified to think that he had been caught in such a scrape, so he

put a hand over his mouth to hide a smile as
he said:

"Of course he isn't going to catch you again.
I know how wise and smart you are, but you
look to me very tired, and there are so many
dangers out here in the Great World that it
seems to me that the very best thing you can
do is to go back to the Smiling Pool."

But Grandfather Frog is stubborn, you
know. He had started out to see the Great
World, and he didn't want the little people of
the Green Meadows and the Green Forest to
think that he was afraid. The truth is, Grandfather Frog was more afraid of being laughed
at than he was of the dangers around him,
which shows just how foolish wise people can
be sometimes. So he shook his head.

"Chugarum!" said he, "I am going to see the
Great World first, and then I am going back to
the Smiling Pool. Do you happen to know
where there is any water? I am very thirsty."

Now over on the other side of the Long
Lane was a spring where Farmer Brown's boy
filled his jug with clear cold water to take
with him to the cornfield when he had to
work there. Striped Chipmunk knew all about
that spring, for he had been there for a drink
many times. So he told Grandfather Frog just

where the spring was and how to get to it. He even offered to show the way, but Grandfather Frog said that he would rather go alone.

"Watch out, Grandfather Frog, and don't fall in, because you might not be able to get out again," warned Striped Chipmunk.

Grandfather Frog looked up sharply to see if Striped Chipmunk was making fun of him. The very idea of any one thinking that he, who had lived in the water all his life, couldn't get out when he pleased! But Striped Chipmunk looked really in earnest, so Grandfather Frog swallowed the quick retort on the tip of his tongue, thanked Striped Chipmunk, and hurried away to look for the spring, for he was very, very thirsty. Besides, he was very, very hot, and he hurried still faster as he thought of the cool bath he would have when he found that spring.

XIX

Grandfather Frog Jumps into More Trouble

SOME PEOPLE are heedless and run into trouble. Some people are stupid and walk into trouble. Grandfather Frog was both heedless and stupid and jumped into trouble. When Striped Chipmunk told him where the spring was, it seemed to him that he couldn't wait to reach it. You see, Grandfather Frog had spent all his life in the Smiling Pool, where he could get a drink whenever he wanted it by just reaching over the edge of his big green lily-pad. Whenever he was too warm, all he had to do was to say "Chug-arum!" and dive head first into the cool water. So he wasn't used to going a long time without water.

Jump, jump, jump! Grandfather Frog was going as fast as ever he could in the direction Striped Chipmunk had pointed out. Every three or four jumps he would stop for just a wee, wee bit of rest, then off he would go again, jump, jump, jump! And each jump was a long one. Peter Rabbit certainly would have been envious if he could have seen those long jumps of Grandfather Frog.

At last the ground began to grow damp. The farther he went, the damper it grew. Presently it became fairly wet, and there was a great deal of soft, cool, wet moss. How good it did feel to Grandfather Frog's poor tired feet!

"Must be I'm 'most there," said Grandfather Frog to himself, as he scrambled up on a big mossy hummock, so as to look around. Right away he saw a little path from the direction of the Long Lane. It led straight past the very hummock on which Grandfather Frog was sitting, and he noticed that where the ground was very soft and wet, old boards had been laid down. That puzzled Grandfather Frog a great deal.

"It's a sure enough path," said he. "But what under the blue, blue sky does any one want to spoil it for by putting those boards there?"

You see, Grandfather Frog likes the soft wet mud, and he couldn't understand how any one, even Farmer Brown's boy, could prefer a hard dry path. Of course he never had worn shoes himself, so he couldn't understand why any one should want dry feet when they could just as well have wet ones. He was still puzzling over it when he heard a sound that made him nearly lose his balance and tumble off the hummock. It was a whistle, the whistle of Farmer Brown's boy! Grandfather Frog knew it right away, because he often had heard it over by the Smiling Pool. The whistle came from over in the Long Lane. Farmer Brown's boy had had his dinner and was on his way back to look for Grandfather Frog where he had been dropped.

Grandfather Frog actually grinned as he thought how surprised Farmer Brown's boy was going to be when he could find no trace of him. Suddenly the smile seemed to freeze on Grandfather Frog's face. That whistle was coming nearer! Farmer Brown's boy had left the Long Lane and was coming along the little path. The truth is, he was coming for a drink at the spring, but Grandfather Frog didn't think of this. He was sure that in some way Farmer Brown's boy had found out which way he had gone and was coming after him. He crouched down as flat as he could on the big hummock and held his breath. Farmer Brown's boy went straight past. Just a few steps beyond, he stopped and knelt down. Peeping through the grass, Grandfather Frog saw him dip up beautiful clear water in an old cup and drink. Then Grandfather Frog knew just where the spring was.

A few minutes later, Farmer Brown's boy

passed again, still whistling, on his way to the Long Lane. Grandfather Frog waited only long enough to be sure that he had really gone. Then, with bigger jumps than ever, he started for the spring. A dozen long jumps, and he could see the water. Two more jumps and then a long jump, and he had landed in the spring with a splash!

"Chugarum!" cried Grandfather Frog. "How good the water feels!"

And all the time, Grandfather Frog had jumped straight into more trouble.

XX

Grandfather Frog Loses Heart

Look before you leap;
The water may be deep.

THAT IS the very best kind of advice, but most people find that out when it is too late. Grandfather Frog did. Of course he had heard that little verse all his life. Indeed, he had been very fond of saying it to those who came to the Smiling Pool to ask his advice. But Grandfather Frog seemed to have left all his wisdom behind him when he left the Smiling Pool to go out into the Great World. You see, it is very hard work for any one whose advice has been sought to turn right around and take advice themselves. So Grandfather Frog had been getting into scrapes ever since he started out on his foolish journey, and now here he was in still another, and he had landed in it head first, with a great splash.

Of course, when he had seen the cool, sparkling water of the spring, it had seemed to him that he just couldn't wait another second to get into it. He was so hot and dry and dreadfully thirsty and uncomfortable! And so—oh, dear me!—Grandfather Frog didn't look at all before he leaped. No, Sir, he didn't! He just dived in with a great long jump. Oh, how good that water felt! For a few minutes he couldn't think of anything else. It was cooler than the water of the Smiling Pool, because, as you know, it was a spring. But it felt all the better for that, and Grandfather Frog just closed his eyes and floated there in pure happiness.

Presently he opened his eyes to look around. Then he blinked them rapidly for a minute or so. He rubbed them to make sure that he saw aright. His heart seemed to sink way, way down towards his toes. "Chugarum!"

exclaimed Grandfather Frog, "Chugarum!"
And after that for a long time he didn't say a
word.

You see, it was this way. All around him
rose perfectly straight smooth walls. He could
look up and see a little of the blue, blue sky
right overhead and whispering leaves of trees
and bushes. Over the edge of the smooth
straight wall grasses were bending. But they
were so far above his head, so dreadfully far!
There wasn't any place to climb out! Grandfather Frog was in a prison! He didn't understand it at all, but it was so.

Of course, Farmer Brown's boy could have
told him all about it. A long time before
Farmer Brown himself had found that spring,
and because the water was so clear and cold
and pure, he had cleared away all the dirt and
rubbish around it. Then he had knocked the
bottom out of a nice clean barrel and had dug
down where the water bubbled up out of the
sand and had set the barrel down in this hole
and had filled in the bottom with clean white
sand for the water to bubble up through.
About half-way up the barrel he had cut a little hole for the water to run out as fast as it
bubbled in at the bottom. Of course the water
never could fill the barrel, because when it
reached that hole, it ran out. This left a

straight, smooth wall up above, a wall alto-gether too high for Grandfather Frog to jump over from the inside.

Poor old Grandfather Frog! He wished more than ever that he never, never had thought of leaving the Smiling Pool to see the Great World. Round and round he swam, but he couldn't see any way out of it. The little hole where the water ran out was too small for him to squeeze through, as he found out by trying and trying. So far as he could see, he had just got to stay there all the rest of his life. Worse still, he knew that Farmer Brown's boy some-times came to the spring for a drink, for he had seen him do it. That meant that the very next time he came, he would find Grandfather Frog, because there was no place to hide. When Grandfather Frog thought of that, he just lost heart. Yes, Sir, he just lost heart. He gave up all hope of ever seeing the Smiling Pool again, and two big tears ran out of his big goggly eyes.

XXI

The Merry Little Breezes Try to Comfort Grandfather Frog

WHEN THE MERRY LITTLE BREEZES of Old Mother West Wind had left Grandfather Frog in the Long Lane where Farmer Brown's boy had dropped him, and had hurried as fast as ever they could to try to find some of his friends to help him, not one of them had been successful. No one was at home, and no one was in any of the places where they usually were to be found. The Merry Little Breezes looked and looked. Then, one by one, they sadly turned back to the Long Lane. They felt so badly that they just hated to go back where they had left Grandfather Frog.

When they got there, they found Striped Chipmunk, who now was scolding Farmer Brown's boy as fast as his tongue could go.

"Where is he?" cried the Merry Little Breezes excitedly.

Striped Chipmunk stopped scolding long enough to point to Farmer Brown's boy, who was hunting in the grass for some trace of Grandfather Frog.

"We don't mean him, you stupid! We can

see him for ourselves. Where's Grandfather Frog?" cried the Merry Little Breezes, all speaking at once.

"I don't know," replied Striped Chipmunk, "and what's more, I don't care!"

Now this wasn't true, for Striped Chipmunk isn't that kind. It was mostly talk, and the Merry Little Breezes knew it. They knew that Striped Chipmunk really thinks a great deal of Grandfather Frog, just as they do. So they pretended not to notice what he said or how put out he seemed. After a while, he told them that he had set Grandfather Frog free and that then he had started for the spring on the other side of the Long Lane. The Merry Little Breezes were delighted to hear the good news, and they said such a lot of nice things to Striped Chipmunk that he quite forgot to scold Farmer Brown's boy. Then they started for the spring, dancing merrily, for they felt sure that there Grandfather Frog was all right, and they expected to find him quite at home.

"Hello, Grandfather Frog!" they shouted, as they peeped into the spring. "How do you like your new home?"

Grandfather Frog made no reply. He just rolled his great goggly eyes up at them, and they were full of tears.

"Why—why—why, Grandfather Frog, what is the matter now?" they cried.

"Chugarum," said Grandfather Frog, and his voice sounded all choky, "I can't get out."

Then they noticed for the first time how straight and smooth the walls of the spring were and how far down Grandfather Frog was, and they knew that he spoke the truth. They tried bending down the grasses that grew around the edge of the spring, but none were long enough to reach the water. If they had stopped to think, they would have known that Grandfather Frog couldn't have climbed up by them, anyway. Then they tried to lift a big stick into the spring, but it was too heavy for them, and they couldn't move it. However, they did manage to blow an old shingle in, and this gave Grandfather Frog something to sit on, so that he began to feel a little better. Then they said all the comforting things they could think of. They told him that no harm could come to him there, unless Farmer Brown's boy should happen to see him.

"That's just what I am afraid of!" croaked Grandfather Frog. "He is sure to see me if he comes for a drink, for there is no place for me to hide."

"Perhaps he won't come," said one of the Little Breezes hopefully.

"If he does come, you can hide under the piece of shingle, and then he won't know you are here at all," said another.

"That's just what I am afraid of!" croaked Grandfather Frog. *Page 78.*

Grandfather Frog brightened up. "That's so!" said he. "That's a good idea, and I'll try it."

Then one of the Merry Little Breezes promised to keep watch for Farmer Brown's boy, and all the others started off on another hunt for some one to help Grandfather Frog out of this new trouble.

XXII

Grandfather Frog's Troubles Grow

> Head first in; no way out;
> It's best to know what you're about!

GRANDFATHER FROG had had plenty of time to realize how very true this is. As he sat on the old shingle which the Merry Little Breezes had blown into the spring where he was a prisoner, he thought a great deal about that little word "if." *If* he hadn't left the Smiling Pool, *if* he hadn't been stubborn and set in his ways, *if* he hadn't been in such a hurry, *if* he had looked to see where he was leaping—well, any one of these *ifs* would have kept him out of his present trouble.

It really wasn't so bad in the spring. That is, it wouldn't have been so bad but for the fear that Farmer Brown's boy might come for a drink and find him there. That was Grandfather Frog's one great fear, and it gave him bad dreams whenever he tried to take a nap. He grew cold all over at the very thought of being caught again by Farmer Brown's boy, and when at last one of the Merry Little Breezes hurried up to tell him that Farmer Brown's boy actually was coming, poor old Grandfather Frog was so frightened that the Merry Little Breeze had to tell him twice to hide under the old shingle as it floated on the water.

At last he got it through his head, and drawing a very long breath, he dived into the water and swam under the old shingle. He was just in time. Yes, Sir, he was just in time. If Farmer Brown's boy hadn't been thinking of something else, he certainly would have noticed the little rings on the water made by Grandfather Frog when he dived in. But he was thinking of something else, and it wasn't until he dipped a cup in for the second time that he even saw the old shingle.

"Hello!" he exclaimed. "That must have blown in since I was here yesterday. We can't have anything like that in our nice spring."

With that he reached out for the old shingle,
and Grandfather Frog, hiding under it, gave
himself up for lost. But the anxious Little
Breeze had been watching sharply and the
instant he saw what Farmer Brown's boy was
going to do, he played the old, old trick of
snatching his hat from his head. The truth is,
he couldn't think of anything else to do.
Farmer Brown's boy grabbed at his hat, and
then, because he was in a hurry and had other
things to do, he started off without once
thinking of the old shingle again.

"Chugarum!" cried Grandfather Frog, as he
swam out from under the shingle and climbed
up on it, "That certainly was a close call. If I
have many more like it, I certainly shall die of
fright."

Nothing more happened for a long time,
and Grandfather Frog was wondering if it
wouldn't be safe to take a nap when he saw
peeping over the edge above him two eyes.
They were greenish yellow eyes, and they
stared and stared. Grandfather Frog stared
and stared back. He just couldn't help it. He
didn't know who they belonged to. He
couldn't remember ever having seen them
before. He was afraid, and yet somehow he
couldn't make up his mind to jump. He stared
so hard at the eyes that he didn't notice a long

furry paw slowly, very slowly, reaching down towards him. Nearer it crept and nearer. Then suddenly it moved like a flash. Grandfather Frog felt sharp claws in his white and yellow waistcoat, and before he could even open his mouth to cry "Chugarum," he was sent flying through the air and landed on his back in the grass. Pounce! Two paws pinned him down, and the greenish yellow eyes were not an inch from his own. They belonged to Black Pussy, Farmer Brown's cat.

XXIII

The Dear Old Smiling Pool Once More

BLACK PUSSY was having a good time. Grandfather Frog wasn't. It was great fun for Black Pussy to slip a paw under Grandfather Frog and toss him up in the air. It was still more fun to pretend to go away, but to hide instead, and the instant Grandfather Frog started off, to pounce upon him and cuff him and roll him about. But there wasn't any fun in it for Grandfather Frog. In the first place,

he didn't know whether or not Black Pussy
liked Frogs to eat, and he was terribly frightened. In the second place, Black Pussy didn't
always cover up her claws, and they pricked
right through Grandfather Frog's white and
yellow waistcoat and hurt, for he is very tender there.

At last Black Pussy grew tired of playing, so
catching up Grandfather Frog in her mouth,
she started along the little path from the
spring to the Long Lane. Grandfather Frog
didn't even kick, which was just as well,
because if he had, Black Pussy would have
held him tighter, and that would have been
very uncomfortable indeed.

"It's all over, and this is the end," moaned
Grandfather Frog. "I'm going to be eaten now.
Oh, why, why did I ever leave the Smiling
Pool?"

Just as Black Pussy slipped into the Long
Lane, Grandfather Frog heard a familiar
sound. It was a whistle, a merry whistle. It
was the whistle of Farmer Brown's boy. It was
coming nearer and nearer. A little bit of hope
began to stir in the heart of Grandfather Frog.
He didn't know just why, but it did. Always
he had been in the greatest fear of Farmer
Brown's boy, but now—well, if Farmer
Brown's boy should take him, he might get

away from him as he did before, but he was
very sure that he never, never could get away
from Black Pussy.

The whistle drew nearer. Black Pussy
stopped. Then she began to make a queer
whirring sound deep down in her throat.

"Hello, Black Pussy! Have you been hunting? Come here and show me what you've
got," cried a voice.

Black Pussy arched up her back and began
to rub against the legs of Farmer Brown's boy,
and all the time the whirring sound in her
throat grew louder and louder. Farmer
Brown's boy stooped down to see what she
had in her mouth.

"Why," he exclaimed, "I do believe this is
the very same old frog that got away from me!
You don't want him, Puss. I'll just put him in
my pocket and take him up to the house by
and by."

With that he took Grandfather Frog from
Black Pussy and dropped him in his pocket.
He patted Black Pussy, called her a smart cat,
and then started on his way, whistling merrily.
It was dark and rather close in that pocket,
but Grandfather Frog didn't mind this. It was
a lot better than feeling sharp teeth and claws
all the time. He wondered how soon they
would reach the house and what would hap-

pen to him then. After what seemed a long, long time, he felt himself swung through the air, and then he landed on the ground with a thump that made him grunt. Farmer Brown's boy had taken off his coat and thrown it down.

The whistling stopped. Everything was quiet. Grandfather Frog waited and listened, but not a sound could he hear. Then he saw a little ray of light creeping into his prison. He squirmed and pushed, and all of a sudden he was out of the pocket. The bright light made him blink. As soon as he could see, he looked to see where he was. Then he rubbed his eyes with both hands and looked again. He wasn't at Farmer Brown's house at all. Where do you think he was? Why, right on the bank of the Smiling Pool, and a little way off was Farmer Brown's boy fishing!

"Chugarum!" cried Grandfather Frog, and it was the loudest, gladdest chugarum that the Smiling Pool ever had heard. "Chugarum!" he cried again, and with a great leap he dived with a splash into the dear old Smiling Pool, which smiled more than ever.

And never again has Grandfather Frog tried to see the Great World. He is quite content to leave it to those who like to dwell there. And since his own wonderful adventures, he has been ready to believe anything he is told about what happens there. Nothing can surprise him, not even the astonishing things that happened to Chatterer the Red Squirrel, about which it takes a whole book to tell.*

THE END.

*NOTE: *The Adventures of Chatterer the Red Squirrel* is available from Dover Publications (0-486-27399-7).